# COMICS SQUAD

## RECESS!

★ **COMICS BY** ★

JENNIFER L. HOLM & MATTHEW HOLM

JARRETT J. KROSOCZKA

DAV PILKEY

DAN SANTAT

RAINA TELGEMEIER & DAVE ROMAN

URSULA VERNON

ERIC WIGHT

GENE LUEN YANG

# COMICS SQUAD
## RECESS!

· EDITED BY ·

JENNIFER L. HOLM, MATTHEW HOLM &
JARRETT J. KROSOCZKA

Better than Pizza Day!

TA-DA!

RANDOM HOUSE NEW YORK

Visit us on the Web! randomhouse.com/kids

Educators and librarians, for a variety of teaching tools, visit us at RHTeachersLibrarians.com

*Library of Congress Cataloging-in-Publication Data*

Comics Squad : recess! / comics by Jarrett J. Krosoczka, Gene Yang, Eric Wight, Jennifer L. Holm and Matthew Holm, Ursula Vernon, Dan Santat, Raina Telgemeier and Dave Roman, Dav Pilkey ; edited by Jennifer L. Holm, Matthew Holm, and Jarrett J. Krosoczka. — First edition.

p. cm.

Summary: "A collection of comics about every kid's favorite school subject: recess" —Provided by publisher

ISBN 978-0-385-37003-5 (trade) — ISBN 978-0-385-37004-2 (lib. bdg.) — ISBN 978-0-385-37005-9 (ebook)

1. School recess breaks—Juvenile fiction. 2. Schools—Juvenile fiction. 3. Humorous stories, American. 4. Children's stories, American. 5. Graphic novels. [1. Graphic novels. 2. Recess—Fiction. 3. Schools—Fiction. 4. Humorous stories. 5. Short stories.] I. Krosoczka, Jarrett. II. Yang, Gene Luen. III. Wight, Eric, 1974– IV. Holm, Jennifer L. V. Holm, Matthew. VI. Vernon, Ursula. VII. Santat, Dan. VIII. Telgemeier, Raina. IX. Roman, Dave. X. Pilkey, Dav, 1966– XI. Title: Recess!

PZ7.7.C658 2014 [Fic]—dc23 2013035223

MANUFACTURED IN CHINA

10 9

First Edition

Random House Children's Books supports the First Amendment and celebrates the right to read.

# ★ CONTENTS ★

I just want to smother these stories in gravy and eat them up!

THEY TOLD ME I'D BE FIRST!

TYPICAL.

C'mon, Babymouse!
Let's get to the comics!
YOU THINK
THERE'LL BE
CUPCAKES?

# THE SUPER-SECRET NINJA CLUB

by

Gene Luen Yang

Any teachers nearby?
Any girls nearby?
Negatory.
Negatory.

On to the first order of business. Jeremy?

Well, seeing as how the holidays are just around the corner, I propose we do a fund-raiser for any ninja among us who might be in need of a new ninja mask.

Hey!

Was that aimed at me? This happens to be my most favorite T-shirt ever!

Well, your favorite T-shirt is as holey as a nun's—!

*Oh. My. GOSH!*

*This. ROCKS!*

Daryl? What're you doing here?

I always knew you guys were awesome, but I didn't know you were *this* awesome! Tell me what you're doing!

*I BEG OF YOU!*

This is a meeting of the Super-Secret Ninja Club.

*No. WAY!*

Shut up! How's it supposed to stay super-secret if you go blabbing about it to Daryl?!

rustle rustle

Listen to me. I've spent my eight long years on this planet wandering from one extra-curricular activity to the next like . . . like some kind of ***extracurricular vagrant***!

I've tried piano, tee ball, roller skating, finger painting . . . none of them fit me. I got so desperate, I even asked my folks to sign me up for a pipe cleaner sculpture class last summer!

BRiiiNG!

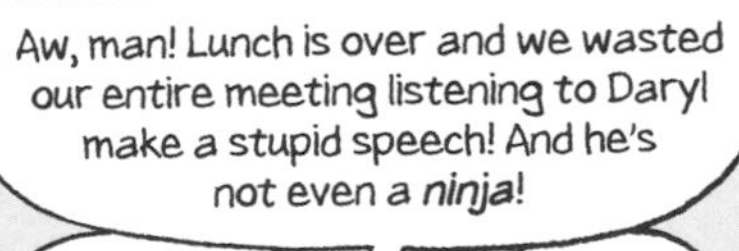
Aw, man! Lunch is over and we wasted our entire meeting listening to Daryl make a stupid speech! And he's not even a *ninja*!

You mean, not a ninja ***yet***!
No, we mean not a ninja ***ever***!

What?! You guys can't do this to me! You can't deny a person his ***destiny***!
Oh, just watch me! I'm about to deny you right in the forehead!

Stop, ***stop***! You guys go to class! I'll handle this!

Go!

Look, Daryl. I would love for you to join the Super-Secret Ninja Club, but you just don't qualify.
Tell me what the qualifications are and I'll meet them, Diego! I swear! My mom says I've got an over-abundance of willpower!
The qualifications are... *sigh* You just have to be a ***super-awesome ninja,*** all right? With ***super-awesome ninja*** skills.
And let's be honest. I've seen you try to jump rope in P.E. You've got ***no*** skills, let alone super-awesome ninja ones.
Not ***yet,*** but I ***will***! I can develop super-awesome ninja skills!
We gotta get to class or we'll be in big trouble. We'll talk more about it tomorrow, okay?
Tomorrow?! But today's the last day before ***Winter Recess***!
Then we'll talk about it after we come back from Winter Recess!
Good idea! That'll give me two weeks to develop my super-awesome ninja skills!

Time to pack up, children! The library's closing for the year. Have a wonderful holiday season!
The eighteen disciplines of the ninja... *This. ROCKS!*
ART OF NINJUTSU

NOE

Discipline #1:
*Seishinteki kyōyō*
Spiritual Refinement
Daryl! Get off the coffee table!

Discipline #2:
*Taijutsu*
Unarmed Combat
Tap out! *TAP OUT!*

Discipline #3:
*Kenjutsu*
Sword Techniques
HIIII-
YAH!

Discipline #4:
*Bōjutsu*
Staff Techniques
HIIII-
YAH!

Discipline #5:
*Sōjutsu*
Spear Techniques
HIIII-
YAH!

Discipline #6:
*Naginatajutsu*
Pole Weapon Techniques
HIIII-
YAH!

Discipline #7:
*Shinobi-iri*
Entering Techniques

Discipline #8:
*Intonjutsu*
Escaping Techniques

Discipline #9:
*Kusarigamajutsu*
Chain Weapon Techniques
Anyone seen the snowflake chain that's supposed to go around the Christmas tree?
HIIII-YAH!

Discipline #10:
*Shurikenjutsu*
Throwing Weapons Techniques
Anyone seen the star that's supposed to go on top of the Christmas tree?
HIIII-YAH!

Discipline #11:
***Kayakujutsu***
Pyrotechnics
Anyone seen the lights that are supposed to be on the outside of the house?
HIIII-YAH!

Discipline #12:
***Hensōjutsu***
Impersonation
Are *you* the true Santa... or am *I*?
?

Discipline #13:
***Bajutsu***
Horsemanship
HIIII-YAH!

Discipline #14:
***Sui-ren***
Water Training
HIIII-YAH!
?

Discipline #15:
*Tenmon*
Meteorology
THE
WEATHER
CHANNEL

Discipline #16:
*Chi-mon*
Geography

Discipline #17:
*Bōryaku*
Political Tactics
THE TIMES

Discipline #18:
*Chōhō*
Espionage
THE TIMES

I hope you had a good Winter Recess, my ninja brothers!
AAH!

Don't be scared! It's me, Daryl!
Oh, hey, Daryl. Why do you have an ugly sweater wrapped around your head?

*Sigh.* I asked for a black T-shirt, but Auntie Lulu got me this instead.

But listen, guys! I did it! It took me two weeks, but *I did it*!

You did what?
I developed *super-awesome ninja skills*! I've become a *super-awesome ninja*! I'm finally ready to join the *SUPER-SECRET NINJA CLUB*!

What are you talking about?

You know, your Super-Secret Ninja Club!
Oh yeah. That was that thing we did for a couple of weeks at the end of last year.

What do you mean, "that thing we did"? Ninjutsu is a ***way of life.***
Ninjas are ***sooo*** last year, Daryl! Everybody's into ***dodgeball*** now!

Dodge-ball?
Yeah. Check out this super-awesome bouncy red ball Chandler got for Hanukkah!
Let's go! Before Daryl makes a speech that takes up the rest of lunchtime!

Maybe if you develop some super-awesome dodgeball skills, we'll let you play with us!

bounce!

POP!

FFFFFFWOOOOSH...

Dodgeball is NOT super-awesome!
FFFWTT...
flop!

Whoa.
Daryl kind of owes me a new ball, but I'm too afraid to ask.

There are **EIGHTEEN DISCIPLINES OF THE NINJA**! Over the next two weeks, I shall train you in *all* of them!

Yes, Sensei Daryl!

Master them, and maybe—*just maybe*—

# MASH-UP MADNESS!

BABYMOUSE LUNCH LADY LUNCH MOUSE

BETTY SQUISH SQUISHETTY

LOCKER FLIPPY BUNNY FLIPPY LOCKER

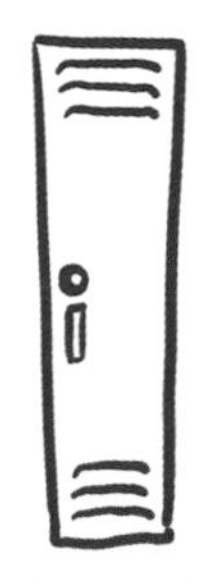

NOW GO TRY DRAWING YOUR OWN MASH-UPS!

a graphic novella

Akshin

LaFFs

FLip-O-Rama

BY George B. and Harold H.

# Jerome Horwitz Elementary School

*We put the "ow" in Knowledge*

Dear Mr. and Mrs. Beard,

Once again I am writing to inform you of your son's disruptive activity in my classroom.

The assignment was to create a WRITTEN public service message to promote reading. Your son and his friend Harold Hutchins (I am sending a nearly identical letter to Harold's mother) were specifically told NOT to make a comic book for this assignment.

As usual, they did exactly what they were told *not* to do (see attached comic book). When I confronted George about his disobedience, he claimed that this was not a comic book, but a "graphic novella." I am getting fed up with George's impudence.

I have told both boys on numerous occasions that the classroom is no place for creativity, yet they continue to make these obnoxious and offensive "comix." As you will see, this comic book contains multiple scenes of stealing, violence, and unlawfulness . . . and don't get me started on the spelling and grammar!

George's silly, disruptive behavior, as well as these increasingly disturbing comic books, are turning my classroom into a zoo. I have spoken to Principal Krupp about *Dog Man* on numerous occasions. We both believe that you should consider psychological counseling for your son, or at the very least some kind of behavior modification drug to cure him of his "creative streak."

Regretfully,

Ms. Construde

Ms. Construde
Grade 1 Teacher

# BOOK 'EM, DOG MAN

By George B. and Harold H.

One day Petey sat in his Jail Cell Feeling sad.

NEWS
DOG MAN Wins again

That Day in the JaiLyard, Petey Got a exscape plan.
MOM

He sat on the see saw...

Yo! BiG Jim! come over and see saw with me!!!
OK!
J

J

weee
J
BONK

So Long, SUCKAS!
CAT JAIL
J

Im Free!

NOW TO Find OUT What makes DOG man so SmarT!

SO PeTer sneaked TO DOG mans HOUSe.

hmm... Hes Reading!

Petey used his Smartometer to check...

DOG MAN was getting smarter by the minute.
Dumb
OK
Supa Dumb
Smart
Jean-yiss

So... Reading makes you smart, eh?

Then I must destroy all BOOKS!!!

One week Later...
Peteys Secrit LAB
You Reeka!

Behold! I JUST invented the word-B-Gone 2000.™

He aimed it at a Book....

ZAP!

iT worked!!! No more words!!!

Petey ran around ZaPP-ing everyThinG in sight.
STOP

Haw Haw!
cRash

Petey Zapped all the Books in the City.
ZAP
Book store

Hey all our Books are Blank!
Book store
Haw Haw

Then he zapped all the Books in the country.
School
Ours Too.
Ours Three
ZAP
PUBLICK LiBarry

Then Petey got in a airplain and zapped all the Books in the whole World!!!
Tee! Hee!
Zap

Before Too Long...
Rats! all The Books on earth are Blank!
aw man!
woe is us!

Soon every Body Forgotted about Reading
OH well
what ever

and People started getting Rilly Dumb!!!
DOY
DOY-eee
Supa DOY!

2 weeks Later...
Awesome!
Peteys secrit LaB

DUMB
OK
Supa DUMB
Smart
Jean Yiss
The world is Supa Dumb!!!

nows my Chanse to have some fun...

Petey walked to the Fansy car Lot.
SALE

Hey, bub!!! Gimme a car!
Duh, my cat had eleven-teen puppies.

Okaaaay...

I'm Just gonna take that one over there!
Duh, my mommy is five years old.

SO Long, SUCka!!!
BYe BYe FroGGY!

The same Thing happend at The Bank . . . . .
Thanks FOr the Free money
DUh, my shoes are Getting married!
JiMS BANK

and The eleck-Tron-icks store.
Thanks For The Free tv!
DUh, This apple Tastes FUNNY!
Jean Yiss

And so...
That was easy!!!

THEN

Yee Haw!

DOG man smelled a cat.

and his "DOG instinkts" Took over.

DOG Man FOLLOWed The Cat SmeLL To Peteys hideout.
Peteys Secrit Lab

he went inside...

...and found Peteys Secrit Stash OF BOOKS.

DOG man started To read...

DOG man Read all nite Long...

...and GOT Smarter and Smarter.

The next morning, DOG man had a plan.
Peteys secrit LaB

He Brought Peteys BOOKS TO The SchooL.
SchooL

and Gaved them TO The kids.

Read, darn ya, Read!!

Soon, Petey woked up...

...To a shock!
My Books!

Petey foll-owed the trail of Books.

it Leaded to the school.
School

Left Hand Here

The See Saw Smoosher

The Swing Set Smacker

The See Saw Smoosher

Spring Break

So Petey Got Capchered...
Rats!

... DOG Man Reversed the word-B-Gone 2000

And soon all The BOOKS on earth got zapped Back to normeL
zap

HORAY FOr DOG Man!!!

# Betty

## and the Perilous Pizza Day

a LUNCH LADY mini-comic

Jarrett J. Krosoczka

I think I have it. . . .

Oatmeal Blaster

SPLATTER!

BOOM!

Lunch Lady, this is Betty, over!

*cough cough* Betty, how did breakfast go?
I'd say it was a big hit! Can't go wrong with waffle tacos!

*cough cough* Betty, I just can't shake this cold. I'm not going to be able to make it in to work today after all. *cough cough*
But today is . . .

PIZZA DAY!

I'm so sorry, Betty. But you're going to have to cover lunch all by yourself.
Roger that, Lunch Lady.

Hundreds of hungry kids on their favorite lunch day of the week!

I'll never make all the pizzas in time!

Unless . . .

It's never been tested, but perhaps the Pizzatron 2000 is my only hope!

WHOOOSH!

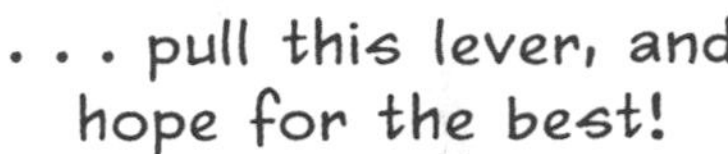

BING!
BANG!
BOONG!
BOOP!

Perfect! Now just a few dozen more and . . .

DING! DANG!
DOONG! DOOP!

BWUAGH!
Nice pizza monster. Down, pizza monster!

BLARGH!

BOOF!

Oh, anchovies!

It's headed
to the cafeteria!

Oh no, you don't! School's in session, yah Cheesenstein!
Trash Lid Shield
Rolling Pin Baton
Where'd it go?!

Hmmm. If I were a bioengineered pizza monster, where would I hide?

Thank green beans, it's recess time.

Otherwise these halls would be crawling with students. But I have exactly five more minutes before that bell rings!

Excuse me, Betty, shouldn't you be in the kitchen getting ready for lunch?!

Uh, hi there, Principal Hernandez!

Just . . . ah . . . getting some exercise in.

Besides, it's Pizza Day! Practically takes care of itself, yah know.

Well, good for you, Betty! You're setting a great example. . . .

The Pizza Monster! I can't let it attack the school's head honcho! My cover will be blown! Ugh! What would Lunch Lady do?!

Principal Hernandez, we have a situation here in the boys' room. Need backup ASAP!

Please don't tell me it's Milmoe again. I'll be right there!

Come on out and play, buddy!
CLANK!

WHOOP!

GROWR!
BAM!
BLOCK!
BONK!

Janitor Kalowski's fan will finish him!
HI-YAH!
BOOF!

Hmmm.
Needs salt.

BRRIIIIIIIIIING!

Yah gotta be kiddin' me!
First the toilets, and now this?
Why is there pizza everywhere?
Hi, yes, I'd like to order a hundred pizzas to be delivered to Thompson Brook School. . . .
THE END

# THE MAGIC ACORN

SCRATCH?!
SCRATCH!

SCRAAAATCH?

URSULA VERNON

SCRATCH!

SCRATCH!
GUESS WHAT?!

HELLO, SQUEAK...
IT'S A MAGIC ACORN! I FOUND A MAGIC ACORN! IT'S MAGIC! AND AN ACORN! COME LOOK! COME LOOK!

RECESS IS OVER IN TEN MINUTES. WE'LL BE LATE.

BUT IT'S A MAGIC ACORN! YOU GOTTA COME SEE!

*SURE*, IT IS.

YOU *PROMISE* WE'LL GO BACK WHEN THE BELL RINGS?

SURE! YES!

SINCE FIRST GRADE, YOU'VE FOUND THREE HUNDRED AND EIGHTEEN "MAGIC ACORNS."

SIXTEEN OF THEM WERE MUSHROOMS...
...FORTY-SEVEN WERE ROCKS...
...ONE WAS A BIRD'S EGG...

AND ALL THE REST WERE *PERFECTLY ORDINARY* ACORNS!
!

BUH...WHUH...?
BUH...?
SEE?! IT'S A MAGIC ACORN!
OH, LOOK! MAGIC ACORN PEOPLE!

HIYA!

I LIKE YOUR ACORN!

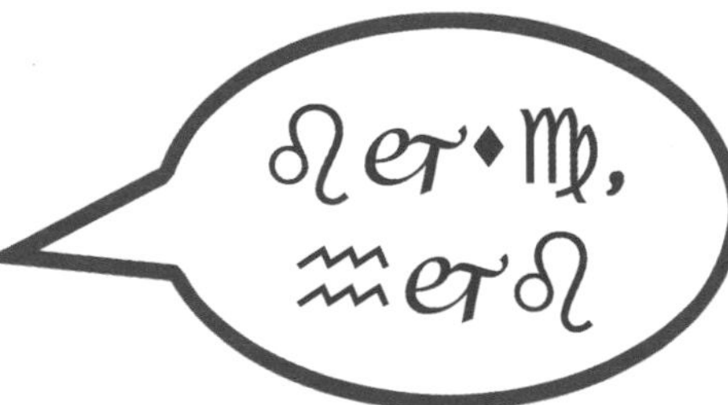

DINGDINGDINGDING!

THAT'S THE RECESS BELL!

C'MON, LET'S GO!

BUH...

WHUH...

BYE! SEE YOU LATER!

WHHHRRRRRRR

BUT...WAIT...

WHERE DID THEY COME FROM? WHY DID THEY LEAVE?!

MAYBE RECESS WAS OVER FOR THEM, TOO.

BUT...
MAGIC ACORN?!
BUT...BUT...
ALIENS!
COOL
MAGIC ACORN,
HUH?
OOH! LOOK,
A MUSHROOM!
GAH!
THE END

WOW! BRING THE ADVENTURE HOME!
Lunch Lady's Home Spy Kit
O.J.
Cereal-O's
You could serve justice and lunch in your very own kitchen!
1. Get your grown-up's permission.
2. Raid the cupboards!
3. Use your imagination to invent your very own Lunch Lady gadgets!

# BABYMOUSE

## THE QUEST FOR RECESS

BY JENNIFER L. HOLM & MATTHEW HOLM

CAMELOT.

THE CUPCAKE TABLE.

WHICH OF THE KNIGHTS OF THE CUPCAKE WILL ACCEPT THIS QUEST?

GULP!

I, BABYMOUSELOT, WILL FIND THE HOLY GRAIL OF RECESS!

NOBLE BABYMOUSE!
BABYMOUSE!
BLINK!
BABYMOUSE!

MONDAY.
BABYMOUSE!
THE BUS JUST WENT BY!
SCHOOL BUS
HUFF
PUFF
VROOOOOOM
THAT'S THE THIRD TIME YOU'VE BEEN LATE THIS MONTH.
NO RECESS FOR YOU TODAY.
YAY!
FORSOOTH.
TYPICAL.
WHEEE!
COMIX R COOL!
READ
HOW'S THAT WHOLE QUEST THING WORKING OUT, BABYMOUSE?

TUESDAY.

GREEK MYTHOLOGY

RECESS WAS SO AWESOME YESTERDAY.

LIKE, EPICALLY AWESOME!

MYTHOLOGICALLY AWESOME!

MOUNT OLYMPUS.

POOF!

WHOA!
WHERE AM I?

MORTAL MOUSE,
YOU ARE IN THE
THRONE ROOM
OF THE
MIGHTY ZEUS!

HUH. I WOULD HAVE THOUGHT THERE'D BE MORE CUPCAKES.
YOU DARE INSULT A MEAN GIRL??
CRACKLE!
HEY! MY WHISKERS!
HA!
CRUMBLE
RING!

BLINK!
RIIINNNNGGG!!!
YOU'RE SAYING YOU'RE LATE FOR CLASS BECAUSE YOU WERE ON MOUNT OLYMPUS AND ZEUS ZAPPED YOU?
LOOK AT MY WHISKERS!
IT'S NEVER WISE TO ANGER THE GREEK GODS, BABYMOUSE.
CRACK!
HMPH.
RECESS
DETENTI
• BABYMOUSE

WEDNESDAY.
EAT YOUR PEAS, PLEASE!

HOW'S YOUR DAY GOING, BABYMOUSE?
GREAT! ONLY TWO PERIODS UNTIL RECESS!

TODAY'S HOT LUNCH IS SPAGHETTI AND MEATBALLS.

MMM! SPAGHETTI!

NOW I JUST NEED TO WRANGLE A SEAT.

THERE WAS A NEW MOUSE AT RECESS.
RRRUUMMMBLE
AND SHE KNEW HER WAY AROUND A LASSO.
CLOP
GALLOP
CLIP
SWIRL
SWOOSH
THEY CALLED HER . . .
BABYMOUSE.
WHIRL
CLOP
CLIP

SWIRL
SWOOSH

TWANG!

BLINK!

TOSS!
SPLAT!

TALK ABOUT A "SPAGHETTI WESTERN."
SIGH.
WHEE!
WHEE!

IN THE HISTORY OF CIVILIZATION . . .

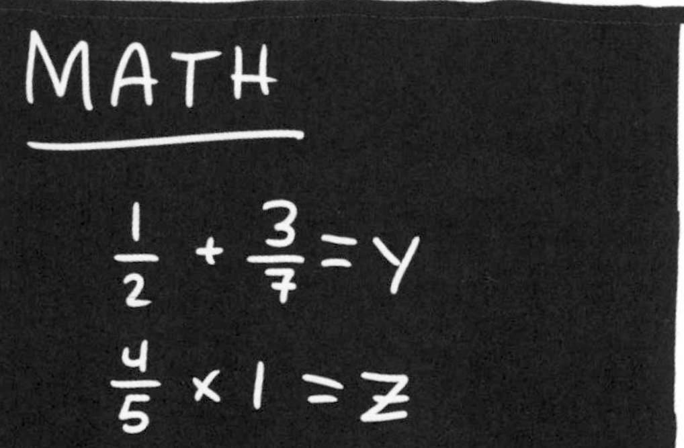

MATH

MARCH MARCH

$\frac{1}{2} + \frac{3}{7} = Y$

$\frac{4}{5} \times 1 = Z$

MATH WAS A NEVER-ENDING BATTLE.

ROME. AD 455.
MARCH
MARCH
MARCH
MARCH
MARCH
CLOP
CLIP
GENERAL BABYMOUSE! THE BARBARIAN FRACTIONS ARE MULTIPLYING!

SWOOSH!
DIVIDE THEM!
AND CARRY THE NUMERATOR!
BABYMOUSE.
CLANG

BLINK!

SORRY, BABYMOUSE.
NO RECESS IF YOU DON'T FINISH YOUR CLASSWORK.

NOW WE KNOW WHY ROME FELL.
RECESS
WHEE!
STUPID FRACTIONS.

ON TIME FOR SCHOOL!

L BUS

DID NOT GET ZAPPED BY LOCKER!

CRACKLE!

SURVIVED LUNCH!

SCRAPE

TRA

FINISHED FRACTIONS!

MATH

FINALLY...
RIIINNNGG!!!
RECESS!!

SCHOOL IS FUN! ☺
ZOOOOOM!

EXIT

GLEAM!

MAYBE YOU SHOULD TRY FOR AN EASIER QUEST NEXT TIME, BABYMOUSE.

KABOOM!

TYPICAL.

THE END

# Jiminy Sprinkles in "FREEZE TAG"

by Eric Wight

Mind if I join you for recess?

...

Sure, I guess so.

Or I can ask someone else if you're not interested.

I'm interested! I'm just not used to having friends. Everyone here thinks I'm a nut.

Grover, but everybody calls me Goober.
Do you like the name Goober?
Not really. But you can still call me it.
So where are you from?
Tons of places. I've moved around a lot.
You're so lucky! I wish I could move somewhere like *New Yolk* or *Cauliflowernia.*
Or pretty much anywhere that isn't here.
Not that here's *such* a bad place...

...as long as you stay away from those guys.

Who are they?

The Mean Green Gang. They think they're so much cooler than everyone else because they're vitamin-fortified.

So much for staying away. They're coming over here!
Oh no! We're *roasted!*

What up, Cake?
H-his name is *Jiminy.*
I can take it from here, Goob—I mean, Grover.

The gang and I were wondering if you'd play Dodge Tag with us.

Sounds fun! Can my friend play, too?
Of course!

See, they're not so bad.

I have a rotten feeling about this.

TAG! You're out!

TAG! You're out!

TAG! You're out!

BOOM went the brussels sprout!
Nobody defeats the Mean Green Gang!
Okay, that was the opposite of fun.
Trying to beat them is fruitless.
Guys, I'm standing right here.
Don't worry. I have an idea.

Hey, Russell! What do you say since we lost that round, we get to pick the next game?
What did you have in mind?
How about Freeze Tag?
I've got no beef with that.
Aw, you never let me be on your team.
First, I need to freshen my breath with this peppermint.

What Russell and the other kids don't realize is that Jiminy is not an *ordinary* talking cupcake.
BE MINE
Eating certain foods causes him to temporarily gain superpowers!

Hope you guys can handle some minty-fresh Freeze Tag!
FROSTY FISTS ACTIVATED!
CHILL OUT!
CHILL OUT!

CHILL OUT!
CHILL OUT!
CHILL OUT!

Whoa! Talk about frozen vegetables!
Don't worry. They'll thaw out in a few seconds.

THE NEXT DAY...
This isn't over, Cake.
Now, take it easy. There's no need to get steamed.
I'm not steamed!
You're not?
That was the best recess EVER!
Check out the giant bag of peppermints I got so we could play Freeze Tag again today!

SPLOOSH!
the end

300 WORDS
by DAN SANTAT
WHAT?! THAT'S DUE TODAY?!
VIDEO GAME

IT WAS ASSIGNED THREE WEEKS AGO.
ARE YOU DONE WITH IT?
I FINISHED IT LAST WEEK.
WHAT AM I GONNA DO?!
RELAX. IT'S 300 WORDS.
GAMECODE

BUT I HAVEN'T EVEN READ THE BOOK YET.

...YOU'RE KIDDING ME...
GAMECODE

JOHN, DID YOU KNOW OUR PAPER ON *THE GIVING TREE* WAS DUE TODAY?
IT IS?! I HAVEN'T EVEN READ THE BOOK YET!

WHAT HAVE YOU TWO BEEN DOING THESE PAST THREE WEEKS?

UH...

THE PAST THREE WEEKS
PEW
PEW
PEW

WHAT AM I GONNA DO?!

SCRIBBLE
SCRIBBLE
SCRIBBLE

"MY BOOK REPORT ABOUT THE GIVING TREE" BY JOHN HARDWICK... ONE-TWO-THREE-FOUR... TEN WORDS!
...YOU'RE NOT SERIOUS...

...HEY, ANDREW, I WAS WONDERING...
NO, YOU CAN'T COPY MY PAPER. YOU CAN LITERALLY READ IT IN TEN MINUTES AND DO IT YOURSELF.
COME ON, I WOULD DO IT FOR YOU.

THAT'S NOT THE POINT! YOU CAN'T GO THROUGH LIFE EXPECTING PEOPLE TO GIVE YOU WHATEVER YOU WANT!

THE STORY IS ABOUT A TREE... IT WAS CALLED THE GIVING TREE BECAUSE IT GAVE STUFF TO PEOPLE...THE TREE WAS BIG AND BUSHY... THIRTY-THREE, THIRTY-FOUR...

THAT IS BEYOND TERRIBLE.
I'M DEAD.
...VERY BIG AND VERY BUSHY... THIRTY-SIX...

HEY, DO YOU THINK SOPHIA WOULD–
NO.
WHY NOT?
ECODE
DUDE. THAT'S MY SISTER.

AND YOU GUYS HAVE A HISTORY. REMEMBER THE SCHOOL PLAY?

THE SCHOOL PLAY

MR. RACCOON, YOU SAVED US FROM THE WOLF! HOW CAN WE EVER REPAY YOU?

BARF!

EEEWWWW

WWWWWW

SHE WAS TEASED FOR WEEKS AFTER THAT, EDDIE. IT WAS HORRIBLE.
YOU PUKED ON HER.

BUT THAT'S WHY IT WOULD WORK! NO ONE WOULD EVER EXPECT SOPHIA WOODSMALL TO LET ME COPY HER HOMEWORK.

YOU NEVER EVEN APOLOGIZED TO HER.

...I MEANT TO... I JUST GET NERVOUS AROUND HER.

I'M GONNA GO ASK HER RIGHT NOW.

HE HAS NO SHAME. DO YOU THINK SHE'LL HELP HIM?
NO WAY. SHE WASHED HER HAIR FOR THREE HOURS THAT NIGHT.

*GURGLE*

UGH. HOLD IT TOGETHER, EDDIE.

HI, EDDIE!
SHHH!

HI, SOPHIA.
HI, ASHA.
WHAT DO YOU WANT, PUKEBOY?

HAHAHA! THAT'S... THAT'S A GOOD ONE, ASHA!... UH, I WAS ACTUALLY JUST COMING TO SAY HI TO SOPHIA.

REALLY? BUT WE NEVER TALK TO EACH OTHER.

YEAH, WELL, I ALSO CAME TO SEE IF YOU DID THE ASSIGNMENT AND MAYBE—

DO YOU NEED TO COPY MY PAPER?
OH. EM. GEE. YOU HAVE SOME NERVE, DUDE.

HERE.
SOPHIA WOODSMALL
THE GIVING TREE

WHAT?! ARE YOU SERIOUS?!

SHE GAVE IT TO HIM!
I CAN'T LET THIS HAPPEN!

WOW! THANKS! I HONESTLY DIDN'T THINK YOU WOULD GIVE THIS TO ME!

ARE YOU OUT OF YOUR MIND?! DID YOU FORGET WHAT THIS GUY DID TO YOU?!

I THINK WE CAN ALL APPRECIATE THE IRONY OF THE SITUATION AFTER READING THE BOOK.

I'M SHOCKED.

I'M DISGUSTED.

UH, I OBVIOUSLY DIDN'T READ THE BOOK.

IN THE STORY A BOY ASKS A TREE FOR THINGS THROUGHOUT HIS ENTIRE LIFE. THE TREE AGREES TO ALL HIS REQUESTS UNTIL HE IS AN OLD MAN AND THE TREE IS JUST A STUMP WITH NOTHING MORE TO GIVE EXCEPT A PLACE TO SIT.

THE BOY WAS SO SELFISH.
I AGREE, HE DID NOTHING FOR THE TREE.

I THINK THE BOY REALLY DID CARE FOR THE TREE. IT WAS NEVER SAID OUT LOUD BUT SOMETIMES I DON'T THINK YOU HAVE TO SAY IT. MAYBE A PERSON DOESN'T HAVE THE COURAGE TO.
I FELT THERE WERE TIMES YOU WANTED TO APOLOGIZE FOR THROWING UP ON ME THAT NIGHT OF THE PLAY, BUT SOMETHING WAS HOLDING YOU BACK.
YOU'RE MY BROTHER'S BEST FRIEND SO I KNOW YOU'RE A GOOD PERSON AND DIDN'T MEAN TO DO WHAT YOU DID. THAT'S WHY I'M GIVING YOU MY HOMEWORK.
THAT AND I THINK YOU'RE ALSO KIND OF CUTE.
GROSS!
YOU COULD DO BETTER!
HEY!

BUT HE'S USING YOU! HE DIDN'T DO ANY OF THE WORK AND HE'S GETTING OFF EASY!

THE END! DONE! 300 WORDS!

I BET THAT PAPER IS AWFUL.
YOU HAVE NO IDEA.

TOUGH LOVE GOT JOHN NOWHERE. WE MIGHT BOTH GET IN TROUBLE IF YOU GET CAUGHT, BUT IN THE END YOU'RE ONLY HURTING YOURSELF BY NOT DOING YOUR OWN WORK.

RIIIIIIING

MOMENTS LATER
I AM TOTALLY ASHAMED OF MY SISTER RIGHT NOW.
I THINK SHE MADE A HUGE MISTAKE.

HOLD ON TO IT. YOU CAN GIVE IT BACK TO ME LATER IN CLASS.

HERE. I DON'T NEED IT. IT'S JUST A STUPID GRADE ANYWAY.

I'M SORRY I THREW UP ON YOU. I SHOULD HAVE SAID SOMETHING BEFORE, BUT I GET NERVOUS AROUND YOU, AND... WELL...

...I THINK YOU'RE CUTE TOO...

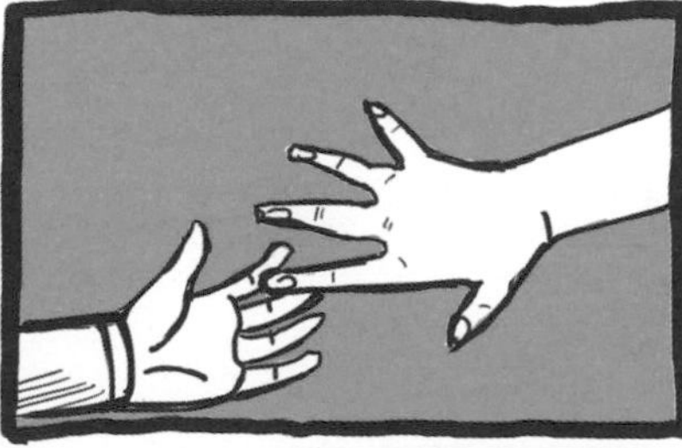

FOR SOPHIA AND ANDREW WOODSMALL

TO ORDER, CALL
1-800-555-0199

ONLY THREE PAIRS LEFT!

THEY SEE EVERYTHING!

MEAN GIRLS!

STORM CLOUDS!

CUPCAKES!

EVEN AMOEBAS!

ORDER NOW AND GET FREE MESSY WHISKERS!

# THE RAINY DAY MONITOR

STORY BY DAVE ROMAN & RAINA TELGEMEIER

ART BY RAINA TELGEMEIER · COLORS BY JOEY WEISER & MICHELE CHIDESTER

MY TEAM'S GONNA KICK YOUR TEAM'S HIDE AT KICKBALL TODAY!

DREAM ON, JOSH.
MY TEAM'S TWO FOR TWO.
YOU DON'T HAVE A CHANCE.
YOU'LL SEE. WE'VE BEEN
PRACTICING, AND WE-
P. J. HAR
BOOM!!
AAAAAAAAAAAAAAAAAAAUGH!!

DO WE **HAVE** TO HAVE A RAINY DAY MONITOR?

**SOMEBODY** HAS TO SUPERVISE YOU GUYS DURING INDOOR RECESS.

BORING BECCA!
Fifth grader
Totally boring

ALL RIGHT, YOU KIDS. EVERYBODY JUST FIND SOMETHING **QUIET** TO DO FOR FORTY-FIVE MINUTES, OKAY?
CAN WE READ?

YES, YOU CAN READ.
CAN WE SET UP A GIANT OBSTACLE COURSE?

UH, **NO.** HOW ABOUT A CARD GAME?
THUNK

BOOOOOOOOOOOOOOOOOOOOOOOOOORING.

SIGH . . . WHAT I **REALLY** WANT TO DO IS PLAY KICKBALL.
grumble

HEY, LISTEN . . .

HAVE YOU EVER PLAYED AN RPG? LIKE DUNGEONS AND DRAGONS?
EW, NO!
THAT'S FOR NERDS!

NO, NO. LET'S HAVE YOUR KICKBALL GAME.
Rummage

WE JUST NEED SOME PAPER AND MY SPECIAL DICE.

NOW, CHOOSE YOUR TEAMS.
. . .

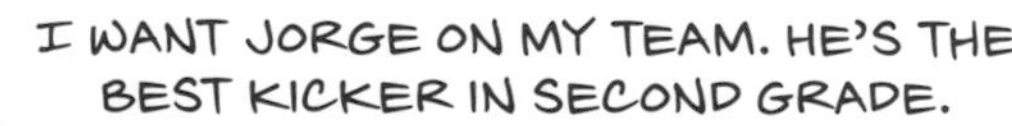
I WANT JORGE ON MY TEAM. HE'S THE BEST KICKER IN SECOND GRADE.

THAT'S WHO YOU'D CHOOSE? THIS IS **IMAGINARY**! YOU CAN CHOOSE **ANYBODY**!
**ANYBODY?!**
OKAY, THEN I CHOOSE . . .

JJ Gutierrez!

The best soccer player in the universe!
Strength +2
Dexterity +4
Charisma +6
06

I ALSO CHOOSE . . .
The President!
Charisma +8
Intelligence +9
Constitution +3

AND . . .
Mr. Iron Ore!!
Metal +10
Mettle+3
Fe

NICE. SONIA?
OH . . .

Dinozilla!!
Strength +30
Intelligence -2
Fire +5

Princess Prickly Pear!
Dexterity +5
Charisma +6
Car Racing +3

Zach from One Dimension!!!
Charisma +50
Intelligence +3
Song +10

NOW . . .
I'M THE DUGOUT MASTER, SO I ROLL THE DICE. . . .

SONIA'S TEAM IS UP FIRST!
LET'S DO THIS!

PRINCESS PRICKLY PEAR IS FIRST UP. HERE COMES THE PITCH. . . .

A KICK! DOUBLE!
WOO!

ZACH KICKS, BUT THE PRESIDENT CATCHES HIS FLY BALL.
LOOK.
Shumph!

DINOZILLA DOESN'T EVEN BOTHER TO KICK—
HE JUST INTIMIDATES THE OTHER TEAM WITH FIRE.

OKAY, OKAY! TWO CONSOLATION POINTS FOR SONIA'S TEAM.

JOSH'S TEAM IS UP. MR. IRON ORE TAKES THE KICKER'S PLATE. . . . HE KICKS . . .

JJ KICKS **ANOTHER** HOME RUN!

DINOZILLA PUNTS. . . .
DOONK!

THE PRESIDENT DIVES FOR THE BALL, AND . . .
. . . 2.

2! HE MISSES!
OOF!

PRINCESS PRICKLY PEAR HOVER-JUMPS TO FIRST BASE, OUT OF MR. IRON ORE'S REACH! OOOOH!

THE PRESIDENT STEPS UP TO HOME PLATE, AND . . . WHAT'S THIS?
BZZ BZZ
HE'S BEEN CALLED AWAY ON CONFIDENTIAL BUSINESS.
WHAT?!
ZOOM
UNITED ST
Fe

WHAT WILL YOU DO NEXT?
UM . . . CALL IN HIS REPLACEMENT?
FIND OUT WHO THAT IS. ROLL!
SEVEN!
IT'S THE VICE PRESIDENT.
SHOULD'VE SEEN THAT COMING.
AW, MAN, THE PRESIDENT WAS **WAY** COOLER!

THE VICE PRESIDENT STEPS UP TO THE PLATE.

HEY, GUYS—
THE RAIN
STOPPED!
YOU CAN GO OUTSIDE FOR
THE LAST TEN MINUTES OF
RECESS, IF YOU LIKE. . . .
NO THANKS, MR. GUFF—
WE WANT TO STAY **INSIDE**!!
THE END

Hey, Squish! Want to learn how to draw Betty in twelve easy steps?

Sounds great! I've always wanted to draw my own comics!

"Draw two circles for her glasses."

1. 

"Next, draw her hat and her perm."

2. 

Whoa! Slow down!

"Now draw her face!"

3. 

"And then the rest of her body!"

12. 

This tutorial is terrible! Look at my drawing!

Sorry! I ran out of room. These pages are small!

# ★★★★ ABOUT THE

## JENNIFER L. HOLM & MATTHEW HOLM

are the brother-sister team behind two graphic novel series, Babymouse and Squish. They grew up reading lots of comics, and they turned out just fine. (babymouse.com)

## JARRETT J. KROSOCZKA

is the author and illustrator of the Lunch Lady graphic novel series, which chronicles the adventures of a spatula-wielding crime fighter. He has been reading and drawing comics since he was a kid, and he turned out all right, too. (studiojjk.com)

## DAV PILKEY

is the author of the phenomenally popular Captain Underpants series. He spent most of his childhood making comics very much like the one in this book. He used to get in big trouble for it at school. Now it's his job. (pilkey.com)

# AUTHORS ★★★★

## DAN SANTAT

spends most of his time writing and illustrating comics and picture books for children. When he's not doing either of those things, he is most likely playing video games or eating. (dantat.com)

## RAINA TELGEMEIER & DAVE ROMAN

are married and live under a pile of comic pages. Raina is the creator of *Smile.* Dave is the creator of the Astronaut Academy series. (goraina.com and yaytime.com)

## URSULA VERNON

writes the comic series Dragonbreath. She still has not learned to tie her shoes correctly. (ursulavernon.com)

## ERIC WIGHT

is the author and illustrator of the Frankie Pickle series. He ate A LOT of cupcakes to get inspiration for his new character, Jiminy Sprinkles. (about.me/ericwight)

## GENE LUEN YANG

began drawing comics in the fifth grade. He hasn't stopped. He's a two-time National Book Award finalist and author-illustrator of the Printz Award–winning graphic novel *American Born Chinese*. (geneyang.com)

# ★ DON'T MISS THESE OTHER GREAT ★ GRAPHIC NOVELS FROM RANDOM HOUSE!

## BABYMOUSE

HER DREAMS ARE BIG! HER IMAGINATION IS WILD!
HER WHISKERS ARE ALWAYS A MESS.

## IT'S GREEN . . . IT'S BLOBBY . . . IT'S GROSS . . . IT'S squish

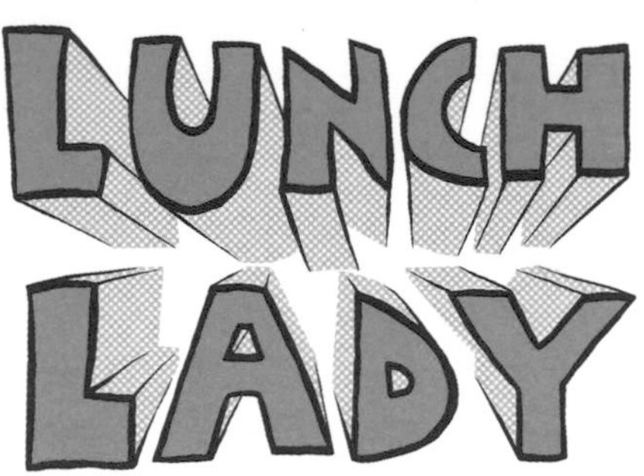


Serving justice! And serving lunch!